ISBN 978-0-9804745-2-7

© Inscrutable Press and the authors, 2016.

inscrutablepress@gmail.com

Design: Michael Blake

Seven Stories

from the Dewhurst Jennings Institute

Edited by Ben Walter

Contents

6

Maps for the Lost
by Susie Greenhill

28

*The Chaos of Life Beyond
Death in the Outback*
by Adam Ouston

37

The Shy Birds
by Emma L Waters

50

An Anti-Glacier Book
by Ben Walter

60

The Reach
by Robbie Arnott

63

Fast Food Librarian
by Ruairi Murphy

78

*Donny and Bucket
on the Treeless Plain*
by Michael Blake

____

Editor's Note

The writers in this anthology, through The Dewhurst
Jennings Institute, won the national Community Writers
Award in 2015. This prize, as part of the Fellowship of
Australian Writers' National Literary Awards, is awarded
for an unpublished manuscript compiled, written and
edited by a group of writers.

The judge's report notes that:

*In the end, the WINNER was the anthology that had
the best writing. Seven Stories was true to its title. It only
contained the short story form and with so few works,
this gave the collection a greater consistency than
any of the other entries...Seven Stories has a distinctly
Australian flavour, not of the flag-waving kind, but with
the simple marriage of place and experience.*

This short anthology represents an opportunity to demonstrate the quality and diversity of emerging Tasmanian fiction writers, many of whom are finding recognition around the country for their work – it is worth noting that the Dewhurst Jennings Institute was the runner-up in this award in the previous year. Inscrutable Press is glad to be able to bring these stories into print.

    – Ben Walter

Maps for the Lost

Susie Greenhill

Most nights, he walks until the dawn light seeps into the laneways of the city, until the industrial drone of street-sweepers fills the calm of Wenceslas Square, and commuters, shops and cafés spill out onto the pavements and lanes of Staré Mesto.

He doesn't remember when it was that the city changed, if there was one fated moment when its spirit – sealed safe beneath the gunnels of a rowing boat – had drifted out, wide into the currents of the Vltava, and left behind a daylight world of vague and soulless beauty. What remains is a city built of surfaces and names: a metropolis of tourist sites, while life retreats into the darkness and the forests.

At midnight, the streets stir with wanderers and thieves, and the river, which pulses through the heart of the city like a question, becomes lithe and glows with moonlight and reflections of stone and lime. Tomaš walks for miles along the banks of the Vltava, through the streets of Mala Strana, and deep into the labyrinthine old town, Staré Mesto, where the names of lanes have changed so many times in the past century alone that becoming lost is inevitable, and vanishing is easy.

It's August, and the late summer heat stretches deep into the night like an east wind, heavy with citrus from the hill gardens of Hradcany. It throws light onto the skin, breath and the curves of his memory where she still lives – where the juice of blood oranges runs down her wrists and into his sleep-heavy mouth, and the skies over Dubrovnik are still clear, the blue world still whole.

*

On the embankment, the leaves of a plane tree, withered with age, are already beginning to turn. The quietest things remind him of her. In Dubrovnik – that distant, circled city – in the first days of autumn he'd moved into her stone flat, high above the street. He'd found work as a diver on the Adriatic coast, and spent most of his days beneath the surface of a sea that seemed to him eternally blue. On weekends, they slept through the heat of the sun, and cooked paella with shellfish from the mouth of the Neretva, bartered from the fishermen who set up their stalls under wide red umbrellas in the shade of the wall.

They were imperfect, tempestuous lovers. They'd moved in together only days after meeting. He had a life in Prague but it paled in comparison to the touch of this clear-hearted, Nereidian girl. Hers was a city of a thousand steps, bitter-orange and almond trees and the delta of an underground river. Their nights were spent rowing between the fishing boats in the harbour, across the broken mirror of the sea.

Iluka woke slowly and spoke in her sleep. She carried armloads of books on the ocean home from the library; photographs of dark chunks of ambergris and cuttlefish papered their bedroom walls. She laughed and cried too easily; it made him feel empty. When they argued, she'd sit reading in the light of the window, twisting her blonde hair unconsciously into a tangled, intractable knot.

They'd listened to the war unfolding around them on the radio in Iluka's room. When the tanks moved into Krajina, and the apartments around theirs had emptied overnight, he'd asked her to come with him, back to his land-locked country in the north. But despite the danger she'd chosen to return to the village of her family in the hills.

For weeks they'd spoken on the telephone, between Prague and Rilje, long into the night. For those moments of talking she seemed warm and close. He'd heard the rain on the roof below the sound of her voice, and her mother crying in the kitchen on the night that Vukovar had fallen. As they spoke, the world around them trembled and cracked. He remembered feeling fractured but impossibly whole. Their love seemed invulnerable.

*

He moves across a footbridge where a streetlight flickers intermittently in the darkness. Further down the river, in an empty car park backing onto the Metro, the sleepless drift between rows of stalls and makeshift cafés. He buys absinthe from an ice-cream van that's lit by candles and dripping with wax, and leans back against a low wall covered in graffiti. The air is heavy with insects and lilac, the heat-scent of cities and unfiltered cigarettes.

Since she disappeared he has found a kind of refuge here, among these nocturnal people. He watches the flow of figures through the market. They have the air of sleepwalkers, a trance-like combination of aimlessness and purpose. He imagines how they'd appear if he could look down on the city from some great height: as if they were marking out invisible maps, or tracing constellations. Perhaps unravelling some fine thread of memory through the darkness.

At the far end of the park, he notices a small crowd gathered in the shadows of a pine hung with strings of paper lanterns and rust-coloured lights. As he walks closer he sees Ivan, an exiled Croat who works with Tomaš' grandfather in the factories on the perimeter of the city. Ivan stands in darkness behind a low, covered table. His audience, mostly junkies and the fearless children who creep between the market stalls like cats, watch intently as he glides his palms across the surface of a great glass jar. Beneath his fingertips, clouds of fireflies move as if his hands were magnetically charged. They glow like satellites, or tiny planets drawn into lilting, elliptical orbit.

When he sees Tomaš, Ivan calls him over to the stall and grips his hand in both of his. For a while they move around the market, talking briefly with acquaintances, trading politics and his grandfather's worn-out jokes. There's a bond of memory, or forgetting, between the two men – one old now, one young – that draws them together but makes both uneasy. As they walk Tomaš notices the trace of sadness in Ivan's low laugh, the way he moves quickly between fragments of conversation, as if some threat were waiting in the silence.

The river slows now, grows silken and eely and dark.
Tomaš smokes a little of Ivan's tobacco, then hesitates
for a moment before reaching into his backpack.

'I've got something you might be interested in,' he
says quietly, unrolling the papers that he passes to his
friend. 'I found this among some old journals of Kolya's...
and I remembered your village wasn't far from Krajina ...?
It's just a poem but it was written before the war began
and I thought perhaps ... I don't know ... I thought of you.
So if you're interested, it's yours.'

Turning from the river, Ivan lifts the papers up into the
light. As he reads, the lines around his grey eyes deepen
in the firelight. Yet for a moment he looks younger;
some distant youth blushes across his face like a lost
friend. He pauses briefly when he's finished reading.
Then, crumpling the poem into the pocket of his jacket,
he walks back to his stall where a small girl is standing,
gazing up at the hypnotic performance of the fireflies.
Ivan smiles down at her and gestures theatrically as he
releases the lid of the jar. The creatures dart upwards,
tracing light above the pine trees and spires of the city
until they vanish like meteors into the night.

*

He walks. In the parklands by the river, the earth-tones
of a violin hang suspended in the night air. The music

moves inside his head. It travels through the full, soft languor of his memories, into the folds and faded cotton of her thin dress with its siren's calls – now fragile, now clear.

Iluka.

The syllables of her name seem to gather like driftwood, like reeds along the rock curves of the riverbed, and nest as swallows – there, and there – beneath the reaches of the Karluv Most.

On the rocks beside the water's edge, still blood-warm with sunlight, he dreams of her village in the hills of central Croatia – the stillness of the mountains and the white, dark mists that fill the ruins of her home. He sees the grapevines and the cypresses, limbs entwined and reaching through the ashen shells of churches; the dew-wet webs that hang like jewels across the blackened hallways. When night falls, packs of grey wolves haunt the bridges and the orchards. Staircases tumble into hanging darkness. Layers of iron and shattered stone sink into the earth.

As he walks, he gathers the corners of his memory together in his arms like some rare gift, some precious and half-remembered dream. Each night he re-imagines the contours of her fate. He pictures her beginning her days in a tower block in some anonymous city, in

Budapest or Istanbul, Zagreb or Berlin. He sees her shaping a new life, a new language, in a fishing village in Leguria, or tending olive-groves and vineyards on the island of Miljet. In his head she swallows salted cheese and calamari pulled from the ocean. She's sleeping, diving deep from polished rocks, running in from the street in unforecasted rain. And every day, as he is, she is forgetting, remembering, beginning again.

*

Traffic lights pass from green to amber to red as he crosses the empty streets. At an intersection close to the centre of town, an old, homeless woman wearing the layered, traditional dress of the country, waits, hunched over, for the lights to change.

It is not a city that displays its wounds. Within the floodlit walls of the old town square, which in daylight is crowded with hawkers and tourists, he pauses by the foot of a statue built to honour a great reformer. Behind him, a beer can rolls into a gutter as stray dogs pull rubbish from a garbage tin. White moths, exhausted by their attraction to the light, fall across the cobblestones like quivering snow. He could remember standing on the edge of this square looking in, with his father, as a child. It was raining. They'd spent the day at his father's office in Nove Mesto, and they stopped to stare through a sea of umbrellas at a brass band playing a fickle salute to the latest, unloved regime. Like the street-names, the monuments of the city tend to change with each passing incarnation. Beside the statue where he sits there's a circle of ground, where the moths lie trembling in the unrelenting light, and the cobblestones are smooth, like the skin across a scar.

*

He walks. To the west, on a street not far from the square, between a marionette theatre and the Chapel of Mirrors, is the library where he works. With the image of the fireflies still in his head, he unlocks a side-door, hidden from the public entrance that faces the street. Inside, after entering a security code, he turns on the lights in the reference hall, three flights of stairs above him.

At night, the building is unheated and dark. Occasionally he meets a security guard or a cleaner on their way to the office, where they drink ink-black coffee and wile away the dusty, soundless hours. Tonight, other than a strip of light beneath the door of a room on the second floor, the building seems to be empty.

For several hours he catalogues the piles of books that have been left unsorted on trolleys, and reshelves the hardbacks the day staff missed. Once in a while

he lets the printed words on the back of a book sleeve
catch his eye, but mostly he tries not to read, or even
pay attention to the titles. His thoughts are only on the
collections of maps in the basement below.

The archives are stored in an underground vault
two flights of stairs beneath the street. The light here
is low and tinged with green. Even at this hour he goes
through the ritual of signing himself in, and puts on
a pair of the filmy gloves that he finds in a box on the
archivist's desk. Outside, a group of pigeons, disturbed
from sleep, re-settle themselves on a window ledge.
One of the projectors used for viewing microfilm has
been left on in a corner; it hums periodically and gives
off a faint and pulsing amber glow.

Along the opposite wall the maps and charts are
secured in steel cabinets. Barely checking the labels –
he has a clear idea of the trays through which he has
already searched – he pulls out one of the drawers.
He lifts aside the sheets of crepe that separate the
parchments, and slides the maps one by one onto the
table before him.

He never knows what it is he's looking for. He feels
an odd affection for the pastel, hand-coloured diagrams
on the page, the way the paper feels heavy against his
palms, and the Gothic illustrations evoking the perils

and charms of exotic lands. The adornments are at once grotesque and naïve, but he knows they were created with calculated skill, and the maps themselves were used as weapons of ruthless, political power. These are not maps that he can carry home and use in his work, they are old, and important, but they lead him towards the kind of maps that are lost or overlooked in the collections of museums.

Time passes, and the sound of a cleaner on the stairs above him breaks his concentration. Glancing at his watch, he slides a street map of Bucharest in a laminated sleeve back into place in the drawer. Still wearing the gloves, like a thief, he leaves the archives and walks back out to the street, and the dark banks of the Vltava.

*

The night grows cold. Across the river, in a quarter of the city where brothels and clubs line a maze of lanes, there's a nightclub he used to go to often with Iluka. He's been there infrequently since returning from Dubrovnik, and other than chance meetings in the city or the market it's the only real contact he has with his friends. They're gentle with him, and it's embedded in their culture to understand the burden of loss, but since she disappeared he feels like the colour has gone from his conversation. At times he feels acutely self-conscious, as though he's been singled out by the floodlights that haunt the inner city. He imagines his grief is visible in his face, like the fine lines that seem to have multiplied during the last difficult months. Even the deeper things they talk of, the philosophy and politics, seem oddly futile, even naïve. It makes him feel old, and for this reason he finds it easier to be alone, or in the company of his grandfather and acquaintances like Ivan.

The tiny club is squeezed into a basement under the street. Because of its complex history, the city is riddled with vaults and tunnels that now house theatres and late-night cafés. Inside, although the low ceiling is illuminated with webs of silver lights, it's almost as dark as it is on the street. The floorboards and the glasses on the tables vibrate with the bass of the German trance. Across the dance floor, in the darkest corner, he sees a group of his friends drinking absinthe shots, stirring teaspoons of molten sugar into tumblers of the wormwood liqueur.

'Tomaš!' They greet him with hugs and drunken kisses. By the bar, Sasha, whom he's known since he was a child, is talking with a girl in a wool dress the shade of the absinthe she drinks. He knows her vaguely through mutual friends.

'Tomaš, this is Virginie, Virginie – Tomaš.' Sasha motions to an empty table and they sit.

'We've met,' Virginie smiles. 'Are you drinking, Tomaš?' Without waiting for his reply she stands and turns back towards the bar. The music gets to him a little. It's too loud and too familiar, but Sasha is a good friend and he feels almost relaxed as he settles into the booth.

'I like her,' Sasha glances back at Virginie. 'We've been out a couple of times. She's a journalist, she writes for the Metro. But how's life, anyway? Are you still working on the map?'

Tomaš nods and slides the ashtray back and forth across the table. Even with Sasha he feels uncomfortable discussing his work.

'I'm getting a couple of shifts at the library, filling shelves after hours. I've just come from there actually.' He shakes his head as Sasha offers his lit cigarette. 'It gives me access to the archives as well ... even at night, which is a bonus.' He rubs his hand across his eyes. 'But I think I'm becoming allergic to dust.'

Virginie returns to the table with three glasses of becherovka, a bitter, herb-based liqueur.

'Are you going to exhibit?' she asks, looking searchingly at Tomaš, as Sasha rests his hand on her knee and takes a drink. 'Sasha told me about your maps.

I know the curator of the Golden through my job, if you're after a contact.'

'Sure, maybe at some stage ...' Aware he sounds elusive, Tomaš tries to avoid her eyes. He wonders how much Sasha has told her about his life. Reaching for his drink, he briefly meets her gaze, but there's something in the way she straightens her dress and smiles that makes the club seem unbearably small. 'To be honest, it's not really that kind of work ... but thanks for the offer.'

The music changes and Virginie pulls Sasha, laughing and mouthing apologies to Tomaš, out onto the dance floor. The bechorovka warms his belly and his throat and he begins to feel light-headed. He goes over to the bar but instead of ordering a drink, he finds himself telling his friends that he's leaving, and despite their protests, moves back up the stairs and into the cool of the quiet street.

*

He walks. By the time he reaches the house, though the city is still in darkness, the street lamps are losing their intensity to the dawn, and the remaining stars and satellites are fading into light. His grandfather, Kolya, who begins his shift at the factory at five, is sitting drinking coffee in the unlit courtyard. Joining him at the table, Tomaš stretches back into his chair and looks up at the sky already streaked with vapour trails, and the silhouettes of the tower blocks closing in around the old stone house.

'I saw Ivan last night,' he takes a mouthful of his grandfather's bitter coffee, 'at the night-market. He asked after you.'

Kolya smiles and, opening a tin of tobacco, rolls his first cigarette of the morning. They sit together in silence. Tomaš tries to stifle a yawn. He can feel his eyes are bloodshot, and can hardly remember the last time he slept. After several minutes, he gets up from the table and goes into his bedroom for a jacket. At the far end of the hall, the small room opens out onto the lane that runs behind the cottage. He pulls a jacket from a basket at the end of his bed. It's a cramped room. Stretched across it, from the corner of the window to the door, there's a clothesline with pages of an atlas pegged out like paper washing drying in the early sun. Next to the bed a cardboard box overflows with old street guides and city plans. There's a compass under the bedside lamp. Diagrams of archaeological digs are scattered across the floor.

Taped on the wall above his father's oak desk is his only photograph of Iluka. The last frame on a disposable camera, its edges are flooded with coloured light. She is sitting in the stern of a rowing boat they'd hired; it looks unstable, as though it's rocking. She's laughing, looking into the lens and clutching the rails as he stands to take the picture. There's a bottle of wine in the bottom of the boat and behind her the city is shrouded in fog, as though trying to hide from the camera's gaze.

In the kitchen, he pours himself the last of the coffee. Their neighbour's wispy, tortoiseshell kitten settles into Kolya's lap. As if out of nowhere, a low jet arcs across the sky with a piercing thunder. It's a frequent event, and one they should have grown used to by now. But watching it from the doorway, Tomaš feels the wood around the door reverberate under his fingers. The coffee ripples in the cup on the table, and the frightened cat disappears over the wall. He thinks of Ivan, who lost his children to the senseless war that still continues in the south, and the fears that he and Kolya have spoken of too often in the past few months pass involuntarily through his mind. He pictures Iluka, there among the ruins of her village, where the pear trees bend their fruit down to her waiting mouth, her hands bandaged and broken. Moving over to his grandfather, he cups his palm on the back of the old man's head, and draws their foreheads together in silence, like a ritual.

'It may not feel like it now,' Kolya whispers, 'but you'll

live through this. I know you will. And if she's alive, it's your art, your magic that will bring her back to us.'

*

The dull glow of a street-light shines into a room cluttered with books and rolls of charts. It's the last night of the summer, and through the open window drifts the music of a radio, barking dogs and traffic and the sweet, uncensored squeals and lazy giggling of a child.

'Art is a secret source of great courage,' his grandfather had told him, on that silver morning when they had woken to find the city papered with posters of ironic, political humour. When every windowpane, train station, monument and streetcar was covered with the images of a revolution, the soft swords that would overthrow a dictatorship. 'There is a power there – for subversion, for sustenance – which can bring strength to any darkness.'

In the half-light, Tomaš clears a space on the desk and glances briefly at the picture on the wall. He unrolls a chart of the Adriatic, scribbled with coordinates and shipping lanes, and anchors it under the weight of books on the corners of the desk. In the centre, pencil lines run across the coasts of a group of diamond-shaped islands. They have quaint, musical names from a time when an old language merged with another. He copies them down on a writing pad, and later will compare them with the titles he finds on the maps in the holdings of the library.

As the room darkens around him, he traces the ridgeline of a long-contested mountain, tracks the geometric lines that carve up a city, the valleys flooded with crimson ink. Some of the charts are moth-eaten in places, or almost translucent from exposure to sun. There are atlases, piled to the ceiling by the door, which are sticky with wood-smoke and coated with dust.

Outside, the sounds of the evening fade and are replaced, one by one, by the sounds of the night. Under his fingers, traces of the buried maps remain visible through the slowly changing layers of the globe. The shadows of continents and a war-torn plateau can still be seen beneath the surface. Tearing out the places that have disappeared from memory, he takes the shapes and names that have been lost to war, to politics, to history, and with a soft brush, pastes them over the surface of the spinning, wooden globe.

The nameless ruins of an abandoned village rest safely on the banks of the wide Miangin River, which flows into a sea of islands, between the thin, volcanic mountains of Kanaky, the atoll of Niulakita. Across the hot and clear subcontinent of Bharat cuts the Saraswati

River. The borders of lost cities are left frayed and overlapping. Czechoslovakia, the country of his parents, and the heart-shaped island of Trowenna – silver-green with middens of shell and stolen tracts of forest – drift, like great ships, over the surfaces of oceans, through a universe of the disappeared, the unaligned, the lost.

Most nights, despite his longing, it's here that she lives – in this borderless Earth.

*

In the midnight-dark, a small crowd gathers around a drum of fire on the Mánesuv Most, listening silently to the brandy-soaked poetry of a cellist. On the edges of the light, a young boy walks slowly. The damp, black nose of a fox cub, cradled in his jacket, peeks out into the air. From the opposite side of the river, Tomaš stops and watches as the boy pulls back the folds of the fabric, and the red fur of the cub shines hot in the firelight.

'The fox is yours for a tenner!' the boy calls out through the darkness, lowering his voice as he crosses the bridge. 'We found him in a warehouse out the back of Hradcany.' He stands for a moment, shifting his weight from foot to foot as if pacifying a baby, and then looks curiously at Tomaš. 'It's up for demolition. We don't know what to do with him. I guess he's most likely better off in the woods somewhere ... but he's yours if you want him.'

The small fox turns his eyes towards Tomaš, and fixes him – there – in his amber gaze, with his molten fear. The night seems to slow and the music fade. Almost without thinking, Tomaš takes his wallet from the pocket of his jeans and crumples the largest of the notes into the boy's outstretched hand. Having nothing with which to hold the cub, he pulls off his jacket, and takes the gently trembling creature in his arms. It's lighter than he imagined, and warm.

In a futile attempt at hiding, the quivering cub pushes his nose into the dark under Tomaš' arm. For a moment, he wonders if he should just put him down and let him go, perhaps release him on the slopes of Petrin Hill. But the fox is so small and young he knows instinctively that it wouldn't survive in the city alone. Slowly at first, without a clear sense of where to go or what it is he should do, he begins to walk, and finds himself heading in the direction of home.

At the house, quietly, so as not to wake Kolya, Tomaš gets his backpack from the cupboard in the hall. Leaving the cub, wrapped in a blanket, in one of the boxes of maps that he empties out onto the bed, he goes into the kitchen and fills two plastic containers with food for himself, and frozen meat for the fox. He leaves a note for his grandfather on the kitchen bench, and slides the photograph of Iluka between the pages of his notebook. With a final look around his bedroom, he ties a rug across his shoulder to form a sling where he cradles the fox, then folding the globe into one of his shirts, he nestles it into the top of his pack and then pulls the drawstring and seals the buckles tight.

He walks towards the river. In moments of darkness, he had imagined taking a boat from the moorings on the riverbank, pushing out and letting go. He'd pictured himself lying against the floor of the boat, letting it drift downstream with the current, and falling asleep to be woken by the sounds of fishing boats out on the open sea.

Among several pulled up in a shallow bend, the boat he chooses is narrow and black, its sharp prow buried in a bank of reeds. Glancing up at the stone path above him, he takes what's left of his cash from his wallet and slides it under the cleat where the boat is tied. Climbing in, clinging tightly to the cub, now whining gently and twisting in his arms, he slips the stern line first and then unties the bow, and lets the night current steer the boat clear of the bank.

At first, when he lets him climb free from the sling, the fox is unsteady on his feet, and hesitant, looking out at the water, but Tomaš feeds him scraps of the thawed meat he has stowed in his pack, and in time he curls up beneath the gunnels and sleeps. Fashioning his jacket and the empty sling into a pillow, Tomaš leans back against the wooden seat. There is little movement on the riverbank, although he knows that in a few hours the night-market will begin, and people will appear between the shadows of the trees.

Despite his work, his knowledge of where the river will take them is hazy. He knows that before they leave the city they'll pass under seven bridges, and that they'll travel first north, then west, through country that's forested and cold. As they drift, he starts to notice the rush of the once silent river that laps beneath the hull, and the faintest constellations appear above them in the widening gaps in the smog. He knows those stars and the river form part of a map, that's moving, and cannot be named. He thinks of Iluka, of the invisible paths that stretch out into the distance. In the backpack, under the paws of the sleeping cub, the earth-globe glows, with hope, with light.

The Chaos of Life Beyond Death in the Outback

Adam Ouston

You decide to fake your own death and start again. You write your own obituary, sign it (for intrigue) in the name of a girl you liked in high school, publish it in the local paper. You take it easy on the adjectives. A dead giveaway. You don't want anyone thinking it's a hoax. You don't want anyone coming after you. Then you vanish. You head for the desert. Because you are from the inner city and haven't hitched before, it takes a while to get the knack. You are nervous. You've heard all the horror stories. But, in the end, you find it surprisingly simple. Your rides come from truckies mainly. You fall asleep, and when you wake up you're not in the Red Centre at all. You're in Kalgoorlie where a filmmaker starts talking to you at the roadhouse. Says he can take you further into the desert. You get into the rented white van that's gone dust-orange and there's a cameraman and a few actors. They have limited equipment, no budget and have been driving west for two days. Normally you'd care about the smell but now you don't know what things you care about and what things you don't. It's as if you're in shock, but you are not in shock. You choose to enjoy the smell. The two actresses are pretty, but this says nothing about them. As the van whips through the blinding zero they tell you they're taking two weeks to scout a location and shoot. They're making a zombie movie called *The Chaos of Life Beyond Death in the Outback* set in one of Western Australia's abandoned gold rush towns. They're yet to decide on which one exactly. Some are too far gone to be useable, and some are still inhabited despite being known as ghost towns. They'll know the right one when they find it. You lie about where you come from. And you lie about your name. Within an hour you're in Coolgardie, and although the Marvel Hotel looks promising, you are soon heading north to Goongarrie. But there is nothing in Goongarrie except an old homestead and a sea of red dirt and tussock. You stop in Menzies for lunch and later stretch your legs at Lake Ballard. The salt flats are vast and inhumane, a desert within a desert or anguish on top of anguish. If not for the birds the landscape would seem anathema to life. In the distance you see what appear to be human figures shimmering in the heat haze. An army as skeletal and grotesque as the survivors of atrocities. Everyone piles out and stands among them. One of the actresses, Djia, calls out your new name. The cameraman takes some wide shots. The director says they can make the statues look like zombies. You say that shouldn't be hard. You continue north. By sunset you are in Kookynie. Before the light fades you tour the silent ruins: the only remaining wall of a municipal building; a crumbling chimney; a decrepit cottage beneath the corpse of an ironbark; an abandoned cemetery and the infinite dust. You are not prepared for the Chinese names on the headstones. Tow Sing Ting. Ah Hen. Wong Miang Jeuk. The guy at the hotel says there are thirteen people living in Kookynie. 'Nineteen tonight,' says the director. He also says that this might be the place. You take three of the six rooms. Two in each. The director and the cameraman want to plan the next few days; they take one of the rooms. And the lead actors want to go over their lines. That leaves you and

Djia. You tell her you'll help with her lines if she wants. You haven't had sex in almost a year and the thought of it makes you panic. At least that's something. Before the obituary you'd even stopped jerking off. Djia says she does not need help with her lines. But she needs to test her products in this heat. She's doing makeup as well as acting. With a shrug of your shoulders you agree. She gets out her kit and does you up. You sit in front of the small, chipped mirror that seems to be stained with tea, and watch your skin turn purple and your eyes yellow and your teeth grey. She's worked on slasher flicks before but she's never done zombies. You can hear the others rehearsing through the walls. And there are footsteps outside, going up and down along the dusty concrete. They sound like boots, heavy-heeled boots grinding into glass. Heel-toe, heel-toe, heel-toe. 'Play dead,' says Djia when she's finished. You lie down on the bed and you are surprised that you are relaxed and you are even more surprised that she fucks you like the devil without removing any of her handiwork. When she goes to the shower you see a vertical scar running between her breasts from the base of her throat to her navel. That night you lie in the dark thinking about friends and family. You don't feel anything. Kookynie turns bad. The director gets punched in the face by one of the thirteen locals. The next few days are spent in the van with everyone's hopes rising and falling at each new town. South to Israelite Bay, through Kanowna, Dundas, Norseman, Buldania and Princess Royal. All deserted but unusable. Some don't even have structures, just street signs and dirt tracks that once might have been roads. And cemeteries. Then there's an argument between the director and the cameraman and you retrace your steps north and further west through 14 Mile, 42 Mile, 45 Mile and Black Flag. Nothing. It's all just red earth and the leftovers of life. There's a day when no one speaks, not even you and Djia despite the fact that you've been making love non-stop. You get out of the van at Gwalia in the Great Victoria Desert, a pinprick of a settlement perched on the lip of a gigantic pit. It's like a gateway to less than nothing. Hell of hells, as if the moon could fall right through it. But the Shire keeps the buildings in peak condition for tourists so it's no good for filming. Every night you hear those heavy boots pacing back and forth outside whatever hotel room you happen to be staying in. You've stopped sleeping and the footsteps appear to be getting louder. When you ask Djia about her scar she says 'Car accident' in a way that makes you not believe her. You head south-west toward Mount Magnet. The director is certain you'll have some luck there. The area is basically a Hollywood set, abandoned towns every few clicks. Everyone is brimming with hope. The van practically levitates. You stop at Kunanalling and manage to do a few scenes around the ruin of the old hotel. The director says he saw you in makeup. He asks you to play the lead zombie instead of him. With a shrug of your shoulders, you agree. Between takes Djia holds your hand. Late in the day she whispers that it wasn't a car accident: she was a child prostitute in Lombok and the scar was a gift from her pimp. She asks you if it bothers you. You say of course not, but to be honest you don't know what bothers you and what doesn't. She calls you by your new name. At 71 Mile there's a broken down tin shed and the bones of a windmill. The leading couple and cameraman go into the shed while the rest of you wail on the walls to signify approaching doom. The screams make you feel uneasy. By night they get a few shots of you stumbling through the darkness, cutting through the van's headlights. It's after twelve a.m. and freezing by the time you're done. Any accommodation is hours away so you huddle together in the van and sleep as best you can. You lie awake listening to the footsteps. A few hours later everyone is woken by a series of wallops on the roof. Possums from the gumtree overhead. No one sleeps after that. So the next day you're all zombies and the cameraman is driving when the van strikes a kangaroo which goes spinning off the highway and into the dust. It isn't quite dead and you can't leave it in pain. The director finds a large rock and brings it down on the animal's head. He has to do it repeatedly because you can still hear it breathing harder after each blow. There's blood everywhere and the director is overly enthusiastic. There's no question in your mind that he's a spoiled child from a wealthy suburb. At the Granites they do a long shot of you under the escarpment feasting at the skull of a silhouette, which in reality is the director. It is always the director, though once or twice it is Djia. 'Don't worry, you won't hurt me,' she says. 'Be as rough as you like,' she says. And then, after another day of empty highways, you strike gold: the intact and abandoned hotel at Big Bell. Red brick and grey concrete. A big old pub like an inland ghostship. Two storeys. Left to crumble, so the sign says, in 1955, by which time the town was completely deserted. Once again you sleep in the van and get to work at dawn. Djia does you up and by midday, when it's almost fifty degrees, everyone is ready. The landscape is vibrating with heat and the white noise of insects. The flies are a menace but they leave you alone. Maybe it's the makeup. The sign says keep out, but despite the cyclone fence and the boarded-up windows you fight your way inside. The sign also says that the pub's bar was once the longest in the land. This is the first room you find. Broken, dusty furniture and fallen beams checker the floor. The bar has collapsed and lies about the place in chunks. There's an old Fosters sign, barely visible through the dust, still fixed to the wall behind the bar. With the scraps the cameraman builds a ladder because the stairs are lethal. You go up to the second level where the bedrooms are. You try to float. The floor could give way any second. The director makes a few passes up and down the hall, bouncing softly as he goes. 'It's OK,' he says. 'It won't collapse.' And when he calls action all your fear evaporates, all your concerns for safety, all your self-consciousness in front of the camera, but also all the blankness, depression and guilt. After all your running: the deluge. Your rampage begins. You bust doors from hinges, smash what furniture remains, break glass and mirrors and rip down cupboards. You are glad that you've spent time with these people. You've grown close. But you are hungry for blood. And so you murder the leading man. And you murder the director. And you murder Djia in a way that makes you feel both sad and happy. And you chase the leading lady in and out of bedrooms, down corridors and through bathrooms. She's good: she has real fear in her eyes. And breaking from convention you get her too. And breaking the fourth wall you turn to the camera and tear its operator limb from limb and feast on the contents of his skull, which is nourishing and warm and revitalising and for once in your life you feel happy. Months later, when they find the camera on the floor and realise your death notice was a hoax, the last thing they see is your undead figure disappearing downstairs leaving behind a ruined set and the sound of your dusty boots grinding through the chaos.

The Shy Birds

Emma L Waters

In the warm shallows of the bay, green threads of seagrass ran. Remnant wake arriving from far away boats. Slow thoughts. Glimmering. From the shadowed side of the bay, workers called out to each other at the oyster farm. Distant as time.

Around the point, outside of the bay, summer crowds were lured by the white sand and aqua jelly ocean rolling in. By mid-morning, it was pocked with footprints and amateur excavations.

Back here, in the salty bay, the shoreline had few inroads and remained undeveloped.

Underfoot, the shredded seagrass dried high on the

shore, meeting crops of samphire in seawater creeks. Caught on tea tree scrub. Down further, the scuff of hard sand. A grey heron turned its head from a branch rising from the rivulet.

I let my feet sink in the sand. Waited and watched. Holes in the sand popped and bubbled with tiny soldier crabs who came and went like buffets of wind. Murmurations of fish flitting through threads of emerald.

You pecked me on the cheek as you passed. Your eyes gleamed and I knew you'd been watching the thousands of tiny fish too.

I hung back. A pair of black and white birds with red beaks pip-pipped anxiously from their sandy tidal island. Shy and nervous. I drew closer. The wind blew. I moved and they flew.

It was quiet again, but for the bodies of small fish as they slipped through the water's grip.

I caught up with you. We left the beached seagrass and found the track, dusty and umber, heading up into the bush. There was a slow slipping through brittle grass. Possibly a snake. More likely a blue tongue.

A kookaburra let out a raspy caw. A year ago on this trail, we'd heard the same hoarse-voiced bird in this patch. There lay the familiar pile of fallen gum limbs in a clearing. We inspected a skeleton with perished flesh and fur clinging. Once a wallaby.

Sun beat strong on the tree trunks of the open bush. A lingering honey and dry spice on the air.

This patch of bush was alive with magic. I could almost hear voices and see figures, like spirits, in the bush. It crackled and glimmered with a mysterious energy. A stillness collecting in small coves.

A short drive away, the township bustled with four-wheel drives towing large white boats, the clinking of slabs being shifted in eager arms, and the clapping of thongs on bitumen car parks.

But this corner was quiet. Birds and insects flecked about. Wrens dotted and strung together errands throughout the bush.

Through dropped grey limbs and razor grass, I left the track to find our swimming spot. Last time, we'd slunk off a crop of rocks into the water. Great orange lichen covered boulders. Today the tide was out. The rocks less inviting, wreathed with yellow-beaded seaweed and sharp black mussels.

There was a loud bang. A shot from back where we'd parked the car.

Then three more.

You looked at me.

We waited. The bush was silenced.

We continued quietly. As the track reunited with the shoreline, the gunshots continued from deep within the bush.

We looked to each other again. The thought occurred to us together – the rifle club up the road.

Another pair of shy birds pip-pipped on the long flat beach ahead. One perched on a proud round rock, the look out for the scout who strode about in the shallows. Prodding for food.

I tried out a few photographs, but it was a wasted effort without a telephoto lens. The birds began pip-pipping to each other urgently and banded together on the rock.

The beach ahead was the loneliest stretch. Mounds of seagrass, banked against close-woven tea tree scrub. At the far end, two schooners were moored, just as they had been last time.

We saw a person walking their dog along the beach. They stopped and sat, small and contained, looking on from a distance as I took pictures. I flipped through the obscure images on the digital screen and deleted all but one. Bothering those shy birds for nothing.

The person remained with their little dog bundled on their lap as we made our way along the shore. It was an interruption to see another person and I knew you felt it too. We never saw people out here.

Two more gunshots rang out in the distance. Then more, with such regularity that it became part of the landscape.

'G'day. How you going?' said the old man.

'Good. Beautiful day,' I said.

A white beard flowed down to his waist.

'Saw you were taking pictures of the pied oystercatchers. There's a nest down the beach a bit. I can show you, if you like. Get some pictures of the eggs?'

He looked up at us from under his floppy brimmed hat, eyes as blue as this day.

I wasn't interested in pictures anymore, but shrugged in the affirmative. He let go of the Jack Russell who took off ahead.

'Thought I'd better hold on to her, or you'd be pissed off with me, scaring away the oystercatchers.'

'They get nervous around people, that's for sure,' I replied.

He considered this without comment and led us along the waterline, dirty white gumboots pushing through the water.

A reticence had come over you and I felt something similar. I kept a conversation afloat.

'Lots of fish around the shore,' I said.

'They're spawning. New moon at the moment.'

He paused. 'New moon? Yes a new moon,' he answered himself and kept walking. 'They come in round the shore where it's warm to breed, away from the other fish who'll eat them.' He stopped and looked up from under his hat. 'Here, you can see them all along here. 'Bout the size of your fingernail.' He indicated his thumbnail. A bitten stub from the sleeve of his oversized, faded to blue jumper.

'Mullet mostly,' he said.

'Yeh, it's amazing what you see if you stop and look around,' I said.

He responded, but I couldn't make out the words.

The rifle shots continued. Steady as footfall.

You hadn't spoken at all. It wasn't like you to hang back.

The old man never gave his name, only that of his dog, Bonnie.

He stopped, pointed high across the bay, keenness in his tone. Then his hand dropped.

'No. I thought it was a sea eagle. You could've taken a picture of that.'

I was irritated by his focus on taking pictures.

The beach was quiet and long. The point, where he'd indicated the nest with the eggs would be, was a way off.

'So, do the sea eagles nest in these trees here?'

I asked, looking up to the dead cradles of gums stretching from the tea tree scrub.

He paused, looking at me for a moment.

'No, on that hill across the bay and the one just back there. I feed them from my boat over there.' To the schooners ahead.

'They've gotten to know you.'

He paused to consider his response.

'Yep, they know they can get a feed. Where'd you park your car?' he asked.

'Just back along the way,' I responded guardedly.

A slight queasiness rose in my gut. I knew that you felt it too. I could almost feel your hand reaching out to hold me back.

The rifles held off. The reverberation of an outboard motor across the water. The tea tree scrub to our left was closed and silent. The birdcalls came from further away, in the bush we'd walked through.

'Eh, Bonnie!' He called out to the quick dog.

Bonnie turned her attention from snuffling the ground and pelted back past us to the edge of the scrub.

'So you know this area well?' he asked.

'Yep, we've been out here a lot,' you replied. A stretch of the truth.

'Local?'

'Both from Tassie, but we live in Melbourne now,' you said, stepping closer.

'Oh, yeh. I've done all that. Gone and come back. Been living on my boat up there for nineteen years. Doing it up slowly. Got the mast down now. Just take my dinghy into town, do a bit of shopping. Whereabouts in Tassie you from?'

'Oh north and south,' you said vaguely.

His dinghy bobbed in the retreating water, up ahead near a jut of rock.

'Where's Bonnie?' I asked.

We paused and looked around.

Bonnie was far behind us, digging about at the edge of the scrub.

'Ah, she's just chasing a lizard. You going all the way around the track today?'

'Nah, just a bit of a walk and head back.'

Last time we'd walked this stretch, a ray had skimmed the shallows, lashed the shore and arced back out to the depths. An electric ripple running through the air, sapping oxygen. Another time I found a ray's skeleton on the beach, cartilage coddled around the spine. Gelatinous sand.

Gunfire repeated.

The old man walked at the lead, head crooked forward, hands disappearing in the long sleeves of his bobbled jumper. I scrutinised the sleeve line, looking for the hard edge of a secreted knife. I knew you were too. Local mythology abounded of curious characters in sleepy seaside towns.

A spring of excitement in his voice, 'Yeh, here's one. Just up here.' He diverted from the waterline, to the top of the narrow beach. White gumboots sinking into the tangle of rotting seagrass. He led us to a drifted grey log and pointed to a small round indent in dry seagrass. Two clasped hands full.

'Yeh, there it is!' He was quite excited now, almost chuckling. He looked up at us, blue eyes bright as he pointed to the empty indent.

'You wouldn't think it to look at it,' he said, 'but just the other week there were eggs in there.'

We looked on uncertainly.

'It's pretty well camouflaged isn't it,' you said.

He inspected the nest. Bonnie sniffed around it and ran ahead.

'They just build them on the ground, and the eggs, well you wouldn't even notice them.'

'Are they small and stripy?' I asked.

He paused and looked at me. His pauses made me

reluctant to speak. Just a stupid out-of-towner.

'No. They're spotty and the size of chicken eggs.'

He indicated with a curled bunch of fingers.

A bearded tennis ball sat in the sand.

'That must be yours,' I said to the dog.

'She might play if you're lucky.'

Bonnie seized the ball in her jaws and ran up to me, spindly tail wagging. She wasn't giving it up.

'You just teasing, are you Bonnie?' I said.

'Only two games she plays, and that's catch and tug of war. She decides which.'

'So, is that it?' you asked.

'No, just up there, in the bush there, there's a nest with eggs in it.'

He scooted up ahead, muttering to himself about pushing the dinghy out so it didn't get beached. I exchanged a glance with you. You gave me a blank face, but I knew you were thinking the same thing. We watched to see if he retrieved anything from the boat.

At the end of the beach, within yelling distance of the two schooners, and just before the track headed bushward, there was a small shed. An outboard motor hung from the lip of a rusted barrel. Ropes and tools lay against its weathered walls. A plywood chopping board lay on a round-headed rock, grey like all beach wood.

Stained with rusty blood.

The old man returned with Bonnie and indicated the track into the bush near the shed. Winding up through an outcrop of oblong rocks. We'd walked it before, but not far in. You stepped in ahead of me behind the old man.

'I hope we can find the nest. It's just up ahead on this point,' he said. The prize of these unhatched shy birds waited for us.

My lungs filled with a heaviness that made it harder to breathe. The queasiness rose in my gut. I didn't know when we would say that we didn't want to go any further. A curdled brew of politeness and paranoia. Born of headlines, gossip, grim tales and being an out-of-towner. I felt myself losing contact with you as you stayed close to the salty-haired old man. I willed you to hold back, but you weren't listening. The air flooded me. I scanned the bush litter for fallen branches. My nerves rose. Bark unfurled in a short gust of wind. The air thickened with insects.

His crooked body in the fleece-lined tracksuit. A hand to the beard. I pictured how I would signal to you that it was time to slip away or make excuses to go. This old man a victim to my racing anxiety. You were just out of arm's reach.

The heaviness rose to my throat.

You broke through with, 'So just up this track a bit further?'

'Just over this little rise here,' said the old man.

You seemed to course with adrenalin. I wanted us to drop back, but you stayed close to him.

The gun fired three times.

A small fishing boat jetted by out in the bay. I turned the crimson camera bag to my side in the hope that it was visible to them. They continued further into the bay.

I looked out across to the oyster farm, but the workers were barely visible. The windows of far-off houses sent pinpricks of sunlight across the water.

The old man was speaking but I couldn't hear him properly. A new fervour in his voice.

We reached the top of the rise. Several fishing rods stuck out of the rocks, lines cast out over the ledge.

A family with two children were set up there. A dinghy bobbing nearby. They looked up, taking in the intrusion.

The old man ambled uncomfortably down the rocky slope, complaining of arthritis. Concerned about the eggs being disturbed.

The heaviness in my chest dissipated as we followed him down.

'You seen the oystercatcher eggs, just sitting there on

the rocks, did you?' he said to the children.

'The eggs are just there,' said the little girl, pointing. 'Two eggs.'

At first we didn't see them, but there they were. Two fawn-coloured, chicken-sized eggs, blotched with darker brown spots, warm in the afternoon sun. I pulled out the camera to take a picture of the eggs, though in truth I wasn't interested in photographing them. I looked up. The old man was retreating with haste back up the rocks.

I called out an uncertain thank you. The words drifted before reaching him as he disappeared into the rise of bush.

The family packed up and returned to their boat.

Within moments we were alone. Two brown eggs at our feet. Standing out on this far flung jut of rock.

An Anti-Glacier Book

Ben Walter

'You know what I say to people when I hear they're writing anti-war books?'

'No. What do you say, Harrison Starr?'

'I say, 'Why don't you write an anti-glacier book instead?'

– Kurt Vonnegut, *Slaughterhouse Five*

All mountains were once seashores. See the gull fossils floating lazily among the updrafts, the warm air billowing from the raised dolerite that fences these ranges; see the sand whipped up with the westerly sleet, the rolling waves flecking up the highland tarns. And all seashores were once mountains. Note the scissored treeline, the rusting trig boats and the sinking dunes, the view blown forcefully into your face. These undulations in landscape

– in time, not in space.

Mock their preference for settled vistas. They climb with seahorses.

Typical, these walkers, counting down hours in the public service, weekends hidden in boots and tents. The good gear – not the latest – crushed into their packs (there are the kids' dentists and they're hoping to visit Vietnam – maybe next year). A trip into the central highlands, the chill mist in the morning scrubbed away by a clear day nodding to forecasts as they follow the dull lake track into the southern reserve; a few hours of moss and waterfalls, centuries of wilderness calendars, occasional breaks in the scrub edging the lake; flat water today, flat and deep. Across the narrow waist, the Traveller Range with Mt. Ida pointing skywards; she has noticed the sun, and even the high peaks are surprised at this bright warmth boiling from the east.

At Echo Point they stop for a bite and a drink. The jetty ramp sinking out into the dense water, a path more certain, intractable. The massive old myrtle disguised as a snow gum, and the old hut, always half-built, the simple bunks and pot-belly stove, the sneaking smell of rats and the small beach so often covered with sun-bathed snow.

Sandwiches stowed in the stomachs, they lurch beneath their packs and tramp towards the lake's north face.

They'll try to climb Mt. Gould tomorrow, hoping the day will swell with weather that makes the summit a gift worth revealing.[1] It's supposed to clag up in the morning, one of those days when the ice creeps between your layers, sending you angry and forlorn and hungry in your head. No views, just a heavy trudge through the thoughtless, slippery cloud, hoping the GPS batteries hold their charge as you retrace your track down the slippery steps collapsing under your feet. There are better days, there are memories.

But today, after stepping down from the junction to Byron Gap, after stomping the hollow boards bridging the saturated plains, they open the stiff door of Narcissus Hut to a library of graffiti, a tangle of arguments and exclamation marks, a thicket of text, bauera blending with scoparia and cutting grass and tea-tree, too great a commotion to press on through, a mass signifying nothing to the walkers' shocked eyes as the woman scrawls another slogan on the calm walls.

They know her face instantly from the broadcasts, her thin figure patrolling the edge of Parliament House, certain and alone, strident in the cameras' grab. Railing,

____

1   So far, a conventional walking story. Little local colour, no raconteur-ish, self-effacing flavour; wouldn't make *Tasmanian Tramp*. They're hoping to climb Gould? What of it? It's been climbed before.

a forceful sentry. Pleading, urging all to consider the damage, the ripping and carving, the great white whales roaring and tearing, the ice blazing into the landscape. Ascribing guilt and judgement; yes, and though erosion fights on many fronts, there's the wind, the breath scouring its annual millimetres of layered stone, there's the water, infiltrating, freezing and flexing, there's the rivers burrowing open tunnels like wombats in the sun, but listen, she would say, her weary grey ponytail leaning against her neck, her sign yelling beside her pernickety voice, as all around the faces whisper together, listen, she would intone as a jaw in the flowing audience drops, laughs, the ice lady, the dumb fucking ice lady, listen, raising her arms, shouting, we must, *they* must absolutely be stopped.[2]

This is the lady met by our walkers,[3] stirring

––––––––

2   She's protesting what? *Glaciers*?

3   …with a few tokens of realism pinched from Pam Clarke. Don't know Pam
    Clarke? In the nineties, she was always on the news. An old lady protesting
    battery chicken farming: the chickens debeaked and sardined in cages
    built for mice, fed ghastly unknowns and blinded into constant egg-
    laying wakefulness. All alone she'd make a stand even as she was mocked
    and abused. I expect the chickens added to the theatre; she certainly
    danced with a two-metre tall hen named Battery Bertha on the steps
    of Parliament House. You can look it up http://www.utas.edu.au/library/
    companion_to_tasmanian_history/C/Pam%20Clarke.htm. One time I believe
    she locked herself in a tiny cage. Maybe she even apparelled herself in
    feathers. I'm not sure, no-one here has bothered with detailed research.
    He's just gathered a few notes to fill out the score, to make this anti-glacier
    woman, this neo-Pam, just a little less thin. The original would be loved these
    days; an archetype of before-her-time. All these foodies who have never
    held a real chicken while it wiggles its wings would be soldiering behind
    her, raising their placards. Picture them breaking into Ingham farms and

up arguments beside one of her alleged ancient battlefields. An apposite location, the scene of the crime. Murder-taping the borders of the national park, stitching up the slopes with cairns.

The walkers think to close the door and pivot on worn legs. They haven't signed up for this tour of deep agendas, and when all is said and done, they're not sympathetic; they love what the glaciers have accomplished, and indeed, that's why they're stalking the shattered dolerite that tumbles around the central reserve. They are not wandering round the gentle fishing country on the east side; who would exchange this landscape made perfect in suffering for the slow, low hills that rise unpersuasively, mimicking the pastoral homelands suburbing the city? Is there something more human or more inhuman in broken, staggering rock? What space does the contrast between valley and peak provide, and which of these landscapes is cowering?

None of this they're planning on discussing, proposing, but she has turned expectantly, she is waiting; will they say anything? Will she? If they turn now, nothing will have happened, nothing at all, and

---

setting the hens free as the executives run around in their moustaches and their flustered suits, scurrying in a wide shot, hopelessly trying to usher the chooks that leap from their hands towards the property gates while the protesters laugh, they laugh; we are watching this groundbreaking Australian film and we laugh, laugh, she's a good woman. She's an icon.

they could camp nearby, fetch water from the river –
they were thinking about using the tent anyway – or
even, there's a couple of hours of daylight left, they
could push on to the plateau, get an early start in the
morning before the weather goes to shit. Might bag up a
few views after all; it would be nice to open up a sunset
on top.

But in truth, they're just a little furious.

Not at the slogans, so much;[4] it's not about her
message. It's that someone has the temerity to be
writing on the walls of Narcissus Hut. If you can
understand: in the parks, the huts are respected as
much as the wildflowers, tarns and alpine scenery.
They are common ground like no other place, not
churches or libraries or cafes. Consolidating all the
functions of shelter in a rough room. There are bridges
and tracks, there are signs; all these are transitory. The
huts gather and express our humanity around a glowing
coal stove.

So while conventional walking etiquette is to keep
your mouth sewn even when someone is pushing
boundaries, a quiet fire on the sandy south west, a

____

4   Not even at the dubious allegories depicting climate change this writer
     seems to be blaring? Come on, stop hiding behind Pam, confess your
     grubby agenda. Do you rather like the idea of tearing up the ice and
     scattering it over the globe?

walking dog loosing its tongue around Ben Lomond –
perhaps mention it in passing to a ranger back where
the roads begin – there's something in this gratuitous
urban behaviour that leads one of the walkers to open
their mouth and ask, What are you doing?

And so they're committed. They take a few steps
inside, drop their packs.

What are you doing, scrawling on the walls of
Narcissus?

She invokes the silence a little longer as the walkers
read the lines folding her cheeks and mouth and
eyes, and then she begins, she makes her case from
the whirlwind even as the sun sends stray visions
into the dark hut. Have you seen the bullet holes, she
asks, have you seen what the flows have done to the
ground? Carving the cirques and moraines that follow
their obese gait? There, she indicates to the south, St.
Clair, the deepest lake in Australia. Know why? It wasn't
flooded for Hydro power, I can tell you. The ice armies
marching, advancing and wiping out the fresh-faced
stones, plucking them from their families and slaving
them downhill, roaring in a battle cry of cracking,
twisting bones. Bulldozing the landscape before
anybody dreamed of damming Pedder. Chiselling the
valleys, deeper and deeper, bleeding the lakes into open

wounds. Pouring blankness over the detailed green. Oh yes, she nods, the faces of the men clear and wary of believing, I know you find it all beautiful, sublime. You'll walk in peace and find yourselves refreshed. A bit stiff afterwards, and sore; though it's not your knees that were drilled clean through. Be thankful they've retreated, sailed off to the south with their invasions. This is a destitute landscape you are walking in, this is a landscape weeping over its brokenness and scars.[5]

It's not so long, but long enough. She stops, throws her marker to the ground and waits for a reaction from the walkers. There is little to say, she has washed across them like a strong southerly, and there is no answer to a southerly, you have to wait until it blows out. They treat her with such precedents in mind. One retrieves the marker, shoves it dutifully into the front of his pack as though it were a piece of rubbish mucking up a campsite.

Can see what you're saying, sure, says the other walker, nodding, consoling.[6] Just maybe don't write your

---

5   What exactly is he getting at? Oh I'm clear there's an *irony*; that wiping out the glaciers has actually become a realistic goal. Vonnegut's kooky analogy – its time has passed. Can't stop wars, can stop glaciers? That's the point?

6   Really? Because I'm still baffled by this text's *redundance*. The glaciers are disappearing anyway; why would anyone need to marshal spirits, advocate and argue for their end? As the glaciers dehydrate, slump over and perish – it's like lobbying for the night to fall. So then. Is the writer *against* climate change, but trying to be artful, less direct than Ian McEwan's *Solar*? That was a terrible book. Or is he melting away our time like so many fat, deceitful texts, grabbing at our minds and slowing us down?

stuff on the walls? Makes its own mess, you see. They are smiling gently, as though she has burst into tears on a long, scrubby climb, tentative, as though she is one of their unbalanced mothers. Yep, nods the walker with the marker locked firmly in his bag, that's right, but you've a right to what you're saying. And I've never looked at it that way before. He goes so far as to briefly broaden his smile.

She is watching them, more passionate than agitated, but slowly her flushed face pools. She walks across and picks up her daypack from the table.

Are you going out with the boat, mate? one walker asks. Shouldn't be too far off, we had a chat this morning at Cynthia Bay, they said there was a decent party coming up. Scout troop, I think.

What then? She has knocked on their door, missioned on their turf, she has said her piece – but they are clearly unpersuaded. They will sleep tonight in the hut, they will boil life into their dehydrated food, sip their port, then sleep long on the flat wooden beds till the discomforts of morning bring them to life, assessing the day, their movements – cups of tea, pissing off the hut's deck. They will climb, if they can, into the old glacial heights, even as she follows the thawed furrow back to Cynthia Bay, the winding Lyell Highway escorting her

to the Hobart coast, to her blogs and her petitions and
her rallies, to her grinding, surplus campaign, while all
around the landscape stretches, leans back in waves
and sand, in mud and in scree, and remembers and
forgets and remembers.[7]

------

7   A strange image I'm left with: an exhibition, photographs of Mawson's
Antarctic huts, the ice pressing in on the door and filling up the rooms,
old mugs, papers...and two books caught and frozen solid, unmoving and
unread.

The Reach

Robbie Arnott

An invisible wire is attached to the point of my chin.

He is playing Lego on the floor beneath me, building a

space shuttle, a castle, a fortress, a pirate ship, and the

wire is dragging my jaw to the right at a slow, even pace.

I try to move my mouth back into shape but it resists,

pushing against my palm, which suddenly feels limp and

watery. We are downstairs in the rumpus room, hiding

from the adults. Now my confusion is joined by pain;

my jaw has reached the physical limit of how far a jaw

can go, cranking an ache into the part of my mandible

that connects to the rest of my skull, and the wire is

still pulling. He is still playing Lego. I see him plugging a brick into the feet of an armour-clad minifigure, possibly a knight, or a soldier, or a ghost-warrior from another dimension – he has become interested in alternate realities lately. The pirates are becoming demon hunters, the cowboys are interstellar voyagers and the fire fighters are *Mad Max* road bandits. I can't keep track of where his mind takes him. I try to tell him about the wire, but it's hard to talk with a yanked jaw. All I can do is gurgle and moan. He looks up, all lips and glares. I am ruining his game. I am always ruining his games. The wire keeps pulling, dragging me to my knees, then to the ground. The world is tilted to ninety degrees, and from somewhere in the middle-distance I feel my limbs flail against his space shuttles, his castles, his fortresses and his pirate ships. I hear him yell, anger and frustration pounding out of his little blond body – yet another smashed masterpiece, yet another broken thought – but I can't see his face, which is the only way to tell how angry he really is. He can do just about anything with his voice – this boy will get work as a voiceover artist on movie trailers or radio ads one day – but I can always gauge the depth of his feeling by the scrunch of his forehead and the heat of his eyes. And now I can only see a sideways version of his folded knees. Spit rolls down my slack cheek. My neck is locked into a rigid column, yet it still manages to whack my temple against the floorboards. An inky cloud starts fuzzing behind my eyes, and I try to touch his pale hand. I reach for him – not with my arm, because that is wedged somewhere out of my control – but I reach nonetheless, although I don't know what with. I reach and twist and writhe through the brittle sea of plastic. And he screams out his rage, surges to his feet and leaves the room, crashing the door closed, drumming his hurt into the stairs as he rises up and away, further and faster, retreating from yet another ruined game, from the unfairness of a brother who breaks and mocks, and I am dark and still and covered in froth.

Fast Food Librarian

Ruairi Murphy

Leaving the Jacksons to complete their flight booking, the librarian strolled across the carpet to where Greg Ashton sat, motionless, staring at his computer screen. As he always did when she came near him, Greg inhaled discreetly through his nose, imagining again her smell in his apartment, on his pillow, his skin.

We talked about this, little lion man. A librarian and a retard. What are you going to be to her? Her pet project? Her monkey? 'How do you spell perfume?' Greg whispered. 'I want to tell ... Tanya that she smells nice.'

They shared a brief, closed smile, after which Greg slowly nodded. Then, like a good monkey, he drew closer the dictionary the librarian placed next to him during every computer help session: performer … performing arts … perfume.

It was the last book Greg ever opened; beyond that afternoon, no words could save him.

*

Alexander Jackson – Ajax to some of his former students – was losing patience. He was haemorrhaging it. He glared at the stalled progress wheel atop the webpage, his credit card details lounging up there on the screen for any illiterate to copy down.

I'll wager someone has frozen the page and is using my identity to buy a dozen dirty movies, the end result of which will be the police kicking down my front door in the middle of the night and parading me out in handcuffs and descending pyjama bottoms. Get an eyeful Mrs Mead! Put that in your bloody community newsletter!

Alex was a firm believer that a purposeful life comprised providing the next generation with the intellectual weapons to survive this world – to what other philosophy could a self-respecting retired teacher subscribe? Without an education of the master narrative, one could hope only to see out their days in poor health, poor spirit, and beneath the feet of those with no greater intelligence than themselves. Alex was aware that the weapons he placed in his students' minds would likely one day be used against him – or worse, against those or that which he believed in. But that was the risk his teachers had mindfully taken on him, and the risk he mindfully repeated.

But my goodness, what manner of weapon is the Internet? This is not a clean, honourable kill. This is torture!

Spoken like a man who knows nothing of true pain and humiliation; well, get ready to receive both.

*

Helen Jackson sat a safe distance from her husband, feigning – as only a good spouse will – something between ignorance and disinterest at his latest defeat by technology. She was, however, not quite removed enough to overlook the familiar fire spreading across the back of his neck.

Ever since Alex's engine – his phrase, infuriating – had momentarily shuddered within his chest, Helen felt as though she actually did look after a car, one she had to fight to give the right fuel, fuss to ensure the odometer ticked over daily, and tune her ear to every rattle and creak, an occurrence of either compelling her to lock it indefinitely in the garage or tow it to a service station.

Helen smiled absently as the librarian came to their rescue yet again. The young woman might have been around the same age as Helen's only daughter, Christine, who had just given birth to a baby girl, Madison. Seven and a half pounds, enormous blue eyes, cute as a kitten … all that remained was to meet this little bundle of joy. *Whatever extra we have to pay the travel agent it's worth it. Do you hear me? I don't want to go to have to see my first granddaughter alone!*

But Helen never got on that plane; how do you celebrate new life when you've sat back and watched it taken from another?

*

Andrea Dodd's fantasy was briefly interrupted as the librarian appeared alongside her to help sort recently-returned books onto a trolley. The two colleagues worked in silence, still in shock at this morning's announcement that their Library would close within the month.

Andrea stole a glance at the crestfallen figure beside her. In spite of years of shrinking budgets, the librarian had advocated tirelessly to preserve this place, one that empowered people, that made them feel safe and welcome, and whose sole purpose was to enrich their quality of life.

The worst part was that those who benefited most raised the least objection. All these people in here today consumed the Library and everyone in it without a second thought. To them the librarian may as well have been a piece of meat, an animal to be slaughtered in front of them that they later mindlessly devoured like a burger in a fast food restaurant.

We're being murdered like livestock right before your eyes and not one of you lifts a finger to stop it! You're to blame for this! If I had my way you'd all be punished in the worst possible ways.

Okay, let's get back to it then ...

*

Keisha Chalmers pushed aside the welcome gate and aimed her double-barrelled stare first at the librarian, then at the other bony bitch behind the counter. Then she spun and laughed at the two girls trailing her. But Lorna Harvey had her head in her phone, and Carrie Dawkins was writing something on the back of Jack Tanner's hand. Keisha didn't even like them anyway. The only reason she hung out with them was that Lorna threw money around and Carrie was trying for her license. Jack was just a leech.

After Keisha unplugged the catalogue computers to charge everyone's phones, Lorna and Jack began sucking face on the youth area couch while Carrie collapsed to the floor and flipped through an old issue of *Dolly*. When Keisha knelt by her friend, Carrie slid the magazine away and told her to go look for a book on the Middle East.

Earlier in the week, during netball, Cynthia Taylor had come up behind Keisha and lifted her by her shorts. The pointing and the laughter had been bad enough, but then everyone started making camel jokes. Hump this, Arabian that. Then just the name: Camel toe.

Whatever, mine's no different to anyone else's. Lorna's has to be worse anyway. Next time we go swimming I'll show them who the camel toe is.

She wouldn't, but close; instead, Keisha soon unmasked everyone in that room.

*

The warmth from the smile that Christopher Pederson shared with the librarian only seconds earlier vanished when he read the handwritten sign beneath the bathroom mirror: 'STRICTLY HAND WASHING BASIN ONLY'. He put his face in his hands. Wasn't it enough that they no longer allowed him to sleep behind the car manuals? Now they wanted to deny him a sink at which to shave?

And you don't need 'strictly' and 'only' for Christ's sake – one or the other carries the same meaning.

When Christopher removed his hands from his face, he was unsurprised to see that his eyes were wet. Shaving was one of the few relics of his old life. He took great care lathering the skin and never rushed the blade, because the face in the mirror that slowly revealed itself might be mistaken for the one that still worked for Shell, that was still married to Sally Pederson, and that still lived in a three-bedroom house on Tolmans Hill. And if the eyes could be deceived, then why not the mind?

I'll just walk out that door and there she'll be. Sally will kiss me and put her arm around my waist. Together, we'll walk home.

But it was a new, much younger ghost that awaited Christopher outside the bathroom that day; he was about to give birth to her.

*

Having laid down an unmatched bid of three no-trump, Henry Kilpatrick excused himself from the table and went looking for the librarian. The Friends of the Library bridge group would shortly pause for morning tea, and the first port of call for the member on tea duty was to collect the kitchen key from the librarian. As he walked, Henry massaged the lump on the left side of the back of his neck. Still painless, and larger than this time last week. A marble, with aspirations of becoming a gobstopper.

Henry considered himself beyond the age where his body repaired. Any damage this late in the hunt was permanent, any growth fatal. But resigned need not mean resignation. Rather than darken one's world, death's shadow might – with the right focus – dilate the pupils enough to see more of its beauty. Speaking of which ...

If I could capture a single image to take with me to the next life it would be an attractive smile. There's nothing quite so disarming, so transporting. This one alone would sustain me through purgatory.

The librarian would feature more than that; the young thing with her arm extended toward him, key in hand, made more beautiful by her smile, would soon *be* Henry's purgatory.

*

Jenny Ward broke step with her mother and walked – at the very edge of a run – past the librarian toward the glass case in the children's area. On the third tier of the case, beside a yellow Transformer, in front of a Superman Deluxe Muscle suit, was a Bratz All Glammed Up Yasmin Doll – *Jennifer's* Bratz All Glammed Up Yasmin Doll.

There were only eight days left in the Summer

Reading Challenge, and Jenny had read one hundred and twenty-two books. That was twelve point two completed Reading Logsheets. She was aiming for one hundred and fifty books – fifteen completed Reading Logsheets!

Jenny held open a nearby book, but her eyes never left her trophy. Purple fur coat, lilac and white top, jeans and pink heels. Three tools to create spiral, crimped, wave, and straight hairstyles. Comes with Glitter Gel for you and the doll!

Mum can't say no anymore if I win one. It's so unfair. She's always treating me like a child.

But Jenny's master plan would have to wait; when the first scream rang out across the Library, it was her mother who rushed to teach Jenny a lesson on how to treat others.

*

Greg was closing his message to Tanya with his standard caveat – 'forgive my spelling but letters swim like fish before my eyes' – when he looked up to see who had screamed. For the moment at least a counter separated the librarian and the teenager, which Greg considered a good thing. The girl's hands were balled, and from between sloping shoulders her head jutted forward, cranking out all manner of filth.

Greg half rose from his chair, but that was as far as he got. *What happens when you lay your hands on her, little lion man? Where will you put those hands? Can you spell lawsuit?*

Yes, I can.

Three days later, after wrapping himself and his Peugeot around a telephone pole, Greg could spell invertebrate, too.

*

Faced with some kind of printing error now, Alex was only too glad of a distraction. But the commotion his eyes settled upon at the Library counter was just further proof that the world you love dies long before you do. Alex remembered a time when you could have belted a kid for behaving like that. No more. They were a protected species now. Even so, even after they stripped him of the cane and later the open hand, he never knew kids to be so brazenly disrespectful. The depravity of the language, the unbridled arrogance, the visceral sense of entitlement – all run of the mill now. All bought, paid for, and swallowed to excess. By whom?

By me. I've learned my place. Back of the line, old man. No argument there. Abject confusion and dismay are no position from which to challenge anything.

Neither is disgrace, and when called upon in a few weeks to meet the challenge of pneumonia, Alex lost.

*

So tuned was Helen's ear to her husband's beat that she only became aware that something was happening when Alex ceased muttering to himself. She had been daydreaming about holding Madison, but now followed his gaze to where that horrible girl was making a spectacle of herself. Absolutely disgusting. That girl and her friends might appear attractive and fun – or at least what passes for such things these days – but Helen knew better. She saw through their shiny veneer to something careless, something cruel, and was unsurprised to see that it had now surfaced and was spilling over.

I remember girls like you. I remember what you are capable of. You are still every bit like the ones I knew when I was young: cheap – cheap and unwholesome. Just you wait until the security guard gets here. Just you wait.

But it was Helen who waited, too long; and who would soon wait again, helpless, while her husband's engine slowly sputtered to a complete stop.

*

Andrea pushed the duress button. She had been

watching Keisha and her friends the second they entered the Library, and now that one of them had flared, she mobilized like a woman ten years younger. She leapt at Keisha from behind, grabbed the girl's shoulders, and, pulling with all her strength, began shouting, 'Let go! Let go of her hair!'

But Keisha was unmoved. For all the girl's apparent vulnerability – the heavy make-up, the silly tie, the oversized shoes – she was made of steel. Andrea continued to pull, but her cry changed:

'Someone please help! Help me!' *I don't understand. Why can't you see what is happening here? How can you all be so heartless?*

Andrea never asked that question again; instead, in the years that followed, she replayed the fight without end, and always to the death.

*

Keisha didn't know what all the fuss was about. Why was this crazy woman on her back? No one else gave a damn. They wanted a piece of it. They were lovin' it.

After she shrugged Andrea to the floor and tightened her grip on the thing in her hands, she looked up and saw Carrie, grinning, pointing her phone. Behind her, Lorna and Jack were grinning too. Keisha grinned back.

They're going to get me right at the end of it. This is

going to be a great clip. Just think how many views I'll get.

Close again, though it wasn't the stunning number of views that later alarmed Keisha; it was the unending visits: fun for the whole family!

*

Christopher emerged from the bathroom a new man, but the hand he ran along his smooth chin abruptly stopped when he saw the eviscerated carcass hanging from the rafters. He'd heard the earlier screams – horrible sounds like a child with their fingers caught in a car door – but assumed a parent would be nearby to intervene. Turns out it was just the librarian. A shame, but hey, that was the natural order of things.

Christopher took a final look at the carcass, nodded at the girl tending it, and went to read the newspapers.

It's business, but unfortunately none of mine. I can only admire girls like that, whose sweat built this great country. God knows I could use a little of that kind of industry myself.

'Industry' wasn't the word the coroner used in her report four months later, but Christopher showed similar initiative to leap from the Tasman Bridge; that, or something chased him off there.

*

Henry was removing the cling wrap from Di Pemberton's cinnamon scones when Caroline Stevenson rose and announced morning tea. As the players approached the serving table, Henry stepped closer to its middle, where a large white plastic urn boiled to a crescendo, then died away again. If anyone asked, he had been carrying that urn – full to the brim – when the screaming began. Never mind that the cries for help continued long after he put it down, nor that his return trips to the kitchen were like walking through a disassembly line, Henry pausing only once to thank the teenage girl with a promise to take her offer of patronage to the bridge committee.

But he needn't have worried. Henry received only one question, from Vernon Price, who, frowning at Mrs Pemberton's scones, looked beyond him toward the door and whispered, 'What smells so damn good out there?'

I imagine it knew little of what was happening anyway. It would have been quick and painless, and then it would have been over.

Not Henry's fate; but even as the lump in his neck swiftly metastasized, he managed a smile or two at the irony of that day – Henry, too, being processed, albeit slower and from the inside out.

*

Jenny sat upright and rigid on a bright yellow lounge chair, her hands folded in her lap and her head turned resolutely toward a bay of encyclopaedias. Her mother sat opposite her, picking from a plate that divided them. Pausing, she told her daughter, 'You might just try one bite.'

Jenny's instinct when the librarian began screaming and struggling had been to run to her. It wasn't right what that older girl was doing. Jenny didn't understand why she thought it wasn't right, but it just wasn't, and she wanted it to stop. On shaking legs, she had managed half a dozen steps forward when the collar of her Laura Ashley blazer tightened around her throat. Her mother's hold was familiar, but the eyes that descended toward hers were so incredulous, the grin below them so bemused, that Jenny didn't immediately recognise her.

You witch! I hate you! I hope you choke on her!

Two weekends later, Jenny celebrated first prize in the last ever Summer Reading Challenge by setting fire to her Bratz doll. After placing the melted remains in her mother's bed, she returned to the Library, picked out a book and a quiet corner, and began to read, slowly.

Donny and Bucket
on the Treeless Plain

Michael Blake

Donny's hand shakes, and Bucket's does not, because

Bucket's hand has nothing to worry about other than

the fact that it's attached to the rest of Bucket, whereas

Donny's hand is attached not just to the rest of Donny

but is also linked – via the blood that scurries invisible

through it and occasionally spurts from it in violent

maroon gouts when Donny gets distracted in the act

of chiselling mortar, which is often – it is also linked to

this whole cascading history of sadness and fear and

despair and atrocity and things so countlessly awful

that it's a wonder there's enough room in such a skin

to hold them, and at the end of the day there probably isn't, which is why they sometimes spill out and have to be drowned or pruned away or obliterated with poisons, or impolitely ignored while they wither and scream and writhe around the filthy linoleum floor, all of which are things that happen to Donny's dad and uncles and cousins and aunties and sisters but not to Donny just yet because he's still young and elastic enough that he can just stretch or bend when such thoughts drop on him or explode or leap out beastlike from behind the fridge when he's going for a piss in the parched two-AM heat on a Sunday night, which is what happened last night and is why Donny is presently asking Bucket about whether they're going to hang out and play Call of Duty tonight or whether Bucket is going to be engaging in his normal Monday night ritual of ruthless self-abuse, to which Bucket says 'Get fucked' and throws a nugget of mortar at him.

Donny's hand shakes and Bucket's does not, because while the bulk of Bucket is stumpy and dumb and forcefully reminiscent of a thing deprived of some critical vitamin during development, he is gifted beyond the elbows with a kind of magical dexterity and ability that the rest of his body lacks the imagination to even dream of, hands deft and strong and hundredfolds cleverer than his brain, they are sure and sharp and the main reason that the two boys have this school-holiday job tapping away with hammer and chisel between two piles of bricks; Donny's tidy and neatly stacked and only occasionally bloodstained and Bucket's looking somehow like they've just come out of the land's own kiln, more bricklike and solid and red and *useful* than even those still clingfilmed and fresh atop the nearby pallet.

Donny's hand shakes and Bucket's does not because while Donny is whip smart and personable and so funny that everyone in town eventually forgets themselves in his presence – letting themselves be carried away on the rising wave of optimism and happiness that lifts any room he happens to be in – the notable exception to these talents is Donny himself, who feels that although people may be weeping with laughter or feeling their brains swell with fresh-cut hope and glorious possibility, this kind of vicarious uplifting assistance is the best he will ever be able to offer, and that a hand in raising the fortunes of others is all he can hope for, because while he would – were it not for his situation – be a candidate for every conceivable kind of success, he was, in his own words, 'Unfortunately born in Ceduna, and even more unfortunately, born a coon in Ceduna.'

His teachers and elders and pretty much everyone except Bucket tell him otherwise, that geography or the colour of his skin are no impediment to achieving his dreams, but Donny is fifteen years old and his certainty is implacable, unassailable, hammered hard by sun and circumstance against the unyielding anvils of the land and his bloodline, so he ignores or rebuts them and all the while works furiously toward ensuring his talents are used as fruitlessly as possible, winning essay competitions and art prizes under pseudonyms and spending the winnings in online economies that fluctuate and tank or never had any value to begin with, and by insistently coming in second-best to Bucket wherever the contest is even vaguely manual, refusing to use brains or charm to gain an advantage over his lumpen friend in anything bar Call of Duty, where he needs every skerrick of guile and nous and gamesmanship to keep the score level, to overcome Bucket's inhuman speed of response and accuracy of thumb.

This is where they live, in the orange dark of Donny's dad's living room, both focused laserlike on the fifty-inch TV, eyes unblinking, thumbs staccato, the occasional snappish sentence of smacktalk the only sound bar gunfire and grenades, this is where these two beings of

pure potential spend the time they own, is where they
waste or burn or weld themselves yet tighter together,
this is where they are when – three kills down, aware
he'll never recover the deficit – Donny throws down his
controller and says 'Check this out.'

Bucket pauses the game in case this is a tactic to
throw him off guard (it's happened before), and looks
to Donny, who holds a postcard before them, an ugly
turquoise-white-and-green affair with a triptych of
coastal scenes clapped between horizontal white
bars and some text that reads 'ESPERANCE, WA –
GATEWAY TO THE ARCHIPELAGO OF DREAMS', which
stumps Bucket on a number of levels, but luckily
Donny is already speaking again, talking about year
ten (Bucket finished last year) and the letter of the law,
and after some time it becomes apparent that Donny
is suggesting they leave, depart, abscond with the old
Falcon stationwagon at the bottom of Bucket's yard
that belonged to his brother who fucked off to the city,
no-one knows which one but the point is that he's not
coming back for an EF Falcon with three mags and a
stodgy plus rust like you wouldn't believe and let's be
honest Bucket, let's look long and hard at this town and
ourselves and ask the really important question here,
which is this, which is 'Who the fuck is going to miss us?

My old man? Your parents? They call, we tell them we've gone up the river camping and by the time they've realised we're not coming back I'm sixteen and there's fuck all they can do. I looked it up, Bucket, we can do what we want and unless we've proven ourselves to be delinquent – which we haven't, we're as close as Ceduna has to model fucking citizens – they can't do jack shit, besides which we'll be a bloody long way away and I'm sure you'll promise to visit them if they're sore.'

Bucket takes his time over his response, given that he's still got one eye on his controller and his memories of Donny's past duplicitous methods of gaining a kill, and the silence is filled with some sort of domestic from the neighbour's yard, although Donny struggles to identify whether it's the occupants of the house or the overloud TV or some combination of both, voices young and old tangling contrarian and confusing against the fence until Bucket says 'Need free.'

Which it turns out is a pretty valid statement, not just literally and metaphorically but – most importantly – on a pragmatic level, because while Bucket holds his learner's permit and Donny can drive, neither of them are qualified to roll alone and their disappearance with the wagon, *sans* licensed adult or legally-viable alternative pilot, would technically constitute an act of delinquency, to say nothing of the actual illegality, and would probably land them back on the coast faster than they would like, or worse, shuffled into some grubby lockup inland, there to be collected by whoever cared enough to make the trek from among their respective families, the exact individual who'd be arriving at the crudely-painted door being decided by a kind of crap-shoot as to who was least wrecked or themselves gaolishly or probatorily inhibited from leaving town, which wouldn't do at all, none of these things would do, Donny seeing his error and already working around it aloud, speaking rapidly of third musketeers and potential candidates and the delicate balance required between headstrength and responsibility, too much of either and they'd be foiled, tossing names and savage character judgements around above the ignored controllers on the floor before finally deciding 'Fuck it, let's just drive around tonight and see who we see.'

Bucket acquiesces, because while disappearing completely in said Falcon is definite grounds for delinquency, driving around town in it is just convenient and he knows most of the cops through his brother anyway, so he's willing to risk the unlikely possibility of a rap on the knuckles if it saves them having to walk through this bloody heat, which they have to do in

the short term anyway, remote-erasing the TV and
stepping out into the griddled streets in their crumbling
trainers, headed for Bucket's parents' place, kicking
a staffy-mauled tennis ball between them, suddenly
sparkling with the simple possible hope of *escape*,
of a future beyond the one they see through cracked
and bleary eyes every morning, that of practicality and
desolation and the kind of nauseous reality that requires
women and men to suffer in equal measure between
rent day and payday and the weekly shop and money
and money and money and time and money and they
know for now that they will have enough of that, both
studious piggybankers saving against some nebulous
future unsurety, they compare notes on hiding places
and favoured denominations and then fall silent as
they pass the block with the bottleshop, where a tired
Australian drama is playing out around the aircon-cooled
exit to the drive-thru, a car parked askance and some
employees looking defensive and a smattering of drunks
(white, black, all ugly) yelling and gesticulating and
doing minor vandalism in the nature strip, in the middle
of it all a woman jigging a baby against her hip and
swearing fit to peel paint and then she is gone, they are
past, forgotten, just quietening echoes bouncing off the
closed shopfronts behind them.

Bucket's house has the same cracked, hopeless slipshod look as the rest of the street, which seems built of cooked earth and dead grass and other things made slightly shittier by heat and salinity, and they don't even bother going inside, kicking their way along through the weeds that sprawl between fence and house, Donny constantly pausing to pick buzzies and grit and leaves from the gutters of his socks, Bucket unfazed and eventually stopping himself to watch, Donny catching his eye and extending his spare middle finger with a 'Fuck you, I hate this shit. You think because I'm black I have to love the bush? A), this isn't the bush, and B), I'm sure I ain't alone, there can't be many people who actually *enjoy* the feeling of grit and a bunch of fucking insects having some dance party in your shoes.'

Bucket's shoulders just lift to his ears, as though to say *Never said that*, and they continue on, dead flora and garbage splintering beneath them, until they arrive at the car and see that the keys are still hanging in it and all the tyres look to be in pretty good shape and but for the petrol gauge, which only rises a bee's dick from its little rest below empty when Bucket reefs the key in the ignition, the rest of it seems okay as well, so Donny goes to wrestle the back gate open while Bucket backs and fills by inches around the back yard until he's content with the alignment of their boatlike conveyance and the gateway and lurches out in a cloud of unburnt hydrocarbons and squeaking brakes, Donny dropping the gate back into the rut between the posts and running out across the tilted footpath to the passenger door hanging open, the hot air inside stale and solid and tasting of cigarettes and motor oil.

They peel out from the kerb, the stodgy on the left-rear skittering and barking until the gearbox makes up its mind and slouches sullenly into second, Donny chuckling and Bucket smiling and though it is tempting to leave them here, two young men in stupid motion and undecided as to whether they care more about accelerating away from their past or toward whatever comes next there's still that pesky thing with the license hanging Damoclean above the whole situation so we'll chase them a while further yet, up to not this intersection but the next, where Donny is already poking his head out the window to ask Ben Hong and Jimmy Inglis what they're doing and who they've seen and whether there's anything going on tonight, nodding sagely and accepting a sip from Jimmy's bottle of flat cola which is predictably sour with bourbon, lowfiving Ben Hong and slapping the side of the car as they pull away again, swishing the dark liquid in his mouth like a soothsayer of old, hunting amongst the froth and sugar for an omen and then swallowing both it and a laugh when Bucket tells him to stop doing that because it sounds disgusting.

For a Monday, town is relatively busy, it being close to peak holiday season plus a few boats are waiting in at Thevenard, so the streets closer to the water are less empty than usual, sunglassed tourists and their yo-yo children looking for something to eat and old people donning visors and sensible footwear in their motorhomes before heading out into the cooling of the evening and the odd local amongst them all, looking for something to do or at least look at in the case of the kids or someone new to have a drink or a chat or a fight with in the case of the adults and through them all Bucket and Donny and the Falcon slide like a rusting torpedo, and they see Deanne Stokes who is no good to them because she just got a job at the pub, and Twig Burnett who's no good because he's still going out with Sharni Ackerley, and Meegan West who's no good because she's a know-it-all, then Ben and Jimmy again, and then they see Krystal Jennings who is no good because both the boys are oddly terrified of her due to her having given Todd Kingston a hand shandy which he described as 'Better than batting it yourself,' a concept which they find confusing and distressing so they just drive by her with a nod and a shared giggle of fright and a block later they see Chelsee Spinks walking her overweight hound and they halt at the kerb beside her and Donny says 'Hey Chelsee, you want to get kidnapped?'

She has headphones in so she doesn't hear him, but she flicks one out and heels the hound and says 'What?' and he repeats himself and she just smiles and asks where they'd be taking her and whether they'd be wanting the dog as well so Donny turns it on and beckons her over and shows her the postcard and then turns not-deadly-but-still-pretty-serious and says 'We're going, Chels. We're getting out,' and leaves it at that, because he has a conman's feel for the weight of decision, and after staring at the card in his hand for what suddenly feels like too long she looks back into his face and sees that he really is offering, catches an edgewise glimpse of his conviction and what it stands upon, and the joke or question or whatever it was she was going to say halts in her throat and she takes out her other earphone and over the tinny whispering of them and the car Donny just looks back and says 'Seriously. Think about it. You've got my number, yeah?' before Bucket's hand – sensing a shudder of importance on some frequency just beyond reach – prods the car into gear and they pull away, the postcard dropping from Donny's fingers to the yellowed grass below, bands of green violent and implausible against the earth and when Chelsee finally looks up and around the inversions hang in her vision like wraiths, leaving her stupid and motionless until the hound pulls at the lead and she starts, shaking her head and glancing down the road again to see if the car is still visible and putting her earbuds back in and only then crouching to pluck the card from the dust and place it in the pocket of her shorts.

In the car they head back to Donny's place, not speaking until they hit the couch and Donny calls for a restart and Bucket laughs and no mention is made of the trip or the card or the third, Donny hopeful and superstitious and Bucket in agreeance, they talk instead of mundanities and nothings and the football and eventually tire and go to bed, Bucket on the couch and Donny in the slum he calls a bedroom, stretched uncomfortable under pilled sheets and the slowly-dulling heat.

The message arrives mid-morning, when Donny is showering and Bucket is eating his second bowl of WeetBix, two words and a punctuation that the shorter boy reads on the upside-down screen of Donny's phone before he slides it under the door into the bathroom for Donny to squint at from behind his still-dripping hair, it says 'Ill come.' and in the brevity of it Donny finds himself almost drunk, awash with the unfamiliar feeling of not speaking or charming but simply having asked quietly and earnestly and being answered and also the realisation that if he wants it this thing will now happen, that nothing barring a mechanical catastrophe will prevent them at least from starting, from leaving, from grasping their savings and what clothes they can carry (which will turn out to be quite a few, in the case of both Chelsee and Bucket) and setting out for the west, and as he dries his hair he pauses with the towel wrapped about his head and his hands to his face, and catches himself between a sob and a laugh and chokes against it and in the end finds himself halfway laughing and crying and still scruffing away at his hair with the towel clenched tight in his tingling hands.

The Writers

Susie Greenhill's short fiction has been published in journals and anthologies including *Island, The Review of Australian Fiction,* the *Overland* ebook *Women's Work, Zoomorphic, Transportation,* and *The Picton Grange Quarterly Review.* She has a PhD in writing and environmental literature from Edith Cowan University, and is writing a novel about extinction and bioluminescent life. She recently won the Richell Prize for her novel *The Clinking.*

Adam Ouston's work has appeared in literary journals, Crikey, Junkee.com, and the 2014 *Transportation: Islands and Cities* anthology. He is the recipient of the 2014 Erica Bell Literary Award for his manuscript *The Party,* which was also shortlisted for the University of Tasmania Prize in the Tasmanian Premier's Literary Awards 2015.

Emma L Waters has written for music press and her short stories have appeared in various journals. She assisted with the first two collections of short stories by small publisher Transportation Press and is also an award-winning songwriter, performing under the name EWAH. After half a lifetime in Melbourne, she calls Tasmania home again.

Ben Walter is a writer of lyrical fiction and poetry who has been widely published in Australian journals, including *Meanjin*, *Island*, *Overland*, *Southerly*, *The Lifted Brow*, and *Griffith Review*. He has twice been shortlisted in the Tasmanian Premier's Literary Prizes, and was the recent guest editor for *Overland's* special anti-/dis-/un-Australian fiction issue.

Robbie Arnott has won the Scribe Nonfiction Prize for Young Writers and the Tasmanian Young Writer's Fellowship, and his work has been widely published in Australia.

Ruairi Murphy is a librarian and writer. His fiction has appeared in journals and anthologies, most notably in *The Third Script: Stories from Iran, Tasmania & the UK*. He lives in Hobart.

Michael Blake is a writer. His work (fiction and non-) has been published locally, nationally and internationally. He was recently shortlisted for the Tasmanian Young Writer's Fellowship.

Previous Publication Credits

'Maps for the Lost' originally appeared in *Etchings* 6.

'The Chaos of Life Beyond Death in the Outback' originally appeared in *Southerly's* The Long Paddock, 74:1.

'An Anti-Glacier Book' originally appeared in *Island* 138, and was accidentally published without its footnotes. These are restored.